Raccoon River Kids
The Third Adventure

ZOOAPALOOZA
in the Park

by Lauren L. Wohl
illustrated by Mark Tuchman

ISBN: 978-1-943978-43-4

Printed in Canada

Library of Congress Cataloging-in-
Publication Data available.

10 9 8 7 6 5 4 3 2 1

CPSIA Tracking Label Information:
Production Location: Friesens Corporation,
Altona, Manitoba, Canada
Production Date: 8/2/2019
Cohort: Batch No. 255074

To six aunts and uncles,

four cousins,

and eight second cousins

with thanks for all the love!

- Lauren

Published by Persnickety Press
An imprint of WunderMill, Inc.
120A North Salem Street
Apex, NC 27502
www.persnickety-press.com

www.WunderMillBooks.com

TUESDAY—THE SECRET STARTS

Lili pulled her arms up as high as she could, and still the doorbell was out of reach. She looked around, found a branch lying in the garden and picked it up. She tried for the bell again – tip of the branch aimed right at the button, arms and body s-t-r-e-t-c-h-e-d to the max. Aha! Lili was rewarded with the sound of the bell coming from inside the house.

Brandon's mom opened the door.

"Hello, Lili." She looked around. "Are you here on your own? Is everything all right?"

"Hello, Mrs. Keefer. Yes, everything's fine. We just

live down the road you know, and my mom said it would be okay for me to walk here by myself." Lili paused for a moment, then asked, "Is Brandon home?"

"He is. He's doing homework. You know where his room is, don't you?"

"Uh-huh. I just have a quick question for him."

Lili walked down the hallway. Brandon heard footsteps, looked out his door and said, "Hey, Lili. Is everything okay?"

"Why is everyone asking that?" Lili leaned closer to Brandon and whispered, "A dog found me."

"Don't you mean that YOU found a dog?" Brandon whispered back.

"Nope. The dog actually found me."

"When? Where? And why are we whispering?"

"After school. It was so nice and warm outside, I was sitting on our front porch, putting new stickers into my album, and this dog came right up to me. I don't know what I'm supposed to do."

Lili stopped for a moment, then added, "We're whispering because my parents can't know."

Brandon wondered what he should say. Lili must be expecting something from him, but he didn't have a clue what it might be. Should he say *wow!* and leave it at that? Or, *what kind?* Or, *does it have a collar?* Or, *what do your parents have against dogs?*

He decided on, "Wow, and does it have a collar?"

Lili shook her head. "No collar. There's no way to know who SHE is and if she belongs to anyone. I bet she does, though, and I'm sure they're missing her right now! Probably looking all over for her."

"Some dogs have a chip that identifies the dog and the owners. Did you check for one?"

"Chip?" Lili asked. "Where would it be?"

"Don't worry about it, Lili. I'll check the dog later," Brandon said. Then he asked, "Where is she now?"

"I made her a house. Kinda. A cardboard box stuffed with an old quilt and pillows so it's cozy. I gave her some milk and some crackers. She seems weak. Do you think she's okay? She's awfully cute."

"Where is the doggie house?"

"In the shed. Even if she barks, no one will hear her. I think she's sleeping. She must have been wandering around for a long time."

"She's probably hungry. And scared."

"Uh-uh. Not scared. She cuddled in my arms and

licked my face. She wants to be my dog. I can tell. I even named her."

Brandon waited.

"Spunky. That's what I call her."

"So, what's the problem? Can't you just keep Spunky?"

"My mother doesn't like dogs. And also, Spunky's family might want her back."

"Good points, Lili."

Brandon turned around in his chair and gave Lili his full attention, pushing his notebook aside.

"How big is Spunky?" he asked.

Lili gestured a size and said, "She's about this long, and she's very fluffy. She looks fat, but it's all hair. Lots of it. She's way smaller than Roxie."

Brandon tried to picture Spunky. He asked, "What color is she?"

"Mostly brown. She has a couple of black spots, too."

"So, you put her in the shed to hide her from your mother?"

"I guess. Just until we figure out what to do."

"*We* huh?"

Lili smiled. "I was hoping you would help."

"I'll do my best, Lili." Brandon thought a moment, then asked, "How come your mother doesn't like dogs?"

"It's not so much that she doesn't like them. She just doesn't want them in our house. She says they are messy. But she says that about everything. She thinks Sunshine, my parakeet, is messy."

"Is Sunshine messy?"

"Sometimes. When she's out of the cage flying around my room, she poops a lot."

Brandon smiled. "Sometimes dogs poop in the wrong places too. Even when they're trained. Roxie has accidents every now and then." Still thinking hard, Brandon asked, "How does your dad feel about dogs?"

"He had a dog. Oswald. He always tells me funny stories about Oswald."

"That's good to know, Lili."

"Why?"

Brandon answered, "He might want to help us."

Lili looked worried, "Oh no. We can't tell him."

Brandon reassured her. "We won't. Not yet anyway."

Brandon had one more question. "How long do you think you can hide the dog before your parents find her?"

Lili put her head down. "Not so long. I don't have food for her. And I don't have money to buy food. I'm only six. Remember?"

"We can do something about the food part." Brandon went into the kitchen. He came back moments later with a giant-sized bag of dog food.

Lili said, "Thank you, but I can't take that Brandon."

"Sure you can! My mom always buys the supersize package. We have plenty for Roxie."

"That's not what I mean. I can't lift this up."

"Right! I'll put some food into a container. Be sure to keep it covered. Tight. Dogs always find their way to where the food is. You don't want Spunky to eat too much and get a belly ache."

"I didn't know dogs get stomach aches. I'll be careful."

Brandon nodded. "Do you have a bowl she can eat from? And one for water?"

"Yup." Then she added, "Thank you, Brandon. Now Spunky won't starve."

"No problem. When you run out of food, bring the container back, and I'll fill it up again. But you know, Lili, this is just temporary. We need to find a real solution—a home for Spunky."

"How do we do that?"

Brandon tapped his index finger against his forehead. "I'm working on it, Lili."

WEDNESDAY—PLAN A

After a quicker-than-usual walk to school, Brandon and Lili hurried to the cafeteria to find their friends Hannah and Nicholas.

"There's Hannah," Brandon said, pointing. "I'm going to talk to her about you-know-what," he told Lili. "I'll meet you in our usual spot after school."

He caught up with Hannah and blurted out Lili's predicament. When Nico joined them, he told the story again, adding "We should help her out."

No surprise! They wanted to get right into action.

"We must know *someone* who wants a dog," Hannah

said. "We should make a list."

"Don't we have to find out if the dog already has a home? If her owners are looking for her?" Brandon asked.

"You're right. We should try to find them first," Nicholas agreed. "Should we go to the police and list the dog as found? Is there even such a thing as a found-dog list?"

Hannah shook her head. "Once the police find out that a first-grader found a dog and is hiding it from her parents, they'll go straight to Lili's house, tell all, and take the puppy away."

Nico and Brandon nodded.

"I promised to keep this a secret. I told Lili we would find a way."

"I wouldn't want to let Lili down," Nico said. "For a little kid, she's pretty spunky."

"So is the dog," Brandon said, grinning. "Lili named the puppy Spunky."

"Do you think your sister could help us out?" Hannah asked Nico. "Take pictures of Spunky to put up around town to see if anyone recognizes her? And maybe get the newspaper to put in an ad or something?"

"I bet she would."

"That would be a good start," Brandon said.

Nico nodded. "Maybe she'll take some pictures tomorrow and send them to the newspaper right away. She can tell them the story and ask for their help."

"Sounds like a plan," Hannah said.

Nico was always home from school before his sister. He waited for her in the kitchen, chomping on chocolate chip cookies, drinking a glass of milk, and tapping his foot on the floor nervously. At last, he heard the front door open.

"Nico?" Melissa called.

"Kitchen," he answered.

"What's that look on your face, Nico?" she said

the moment she saw him at the table. "Do you have something cooking?"

"It's a secret."

"Okay," she encouraged.

"Lili found a dog…" he began.

"And?"

"And it's complicated. We can't tell her parents. Lili wants us kids to try and find the puppy's owners."

"I don't like keeping secrets," Melissa said. "Parents always find out."

"Not if we're quick," Nico said. "We have a plan, but we need your help."

"A new project, I see."

"Guess so," Nico said. "You've always been a part of our projects."

"What are you thinking?" Melissa was getting interested.

"Take a picture of Spunky."

"Spunky?"

"Lili named the dog Spunky."

"Sweet. Sure, I'll take her picture."

"Tomorrow? Right after school? Lili's hiding Spunky in the shed. Behind their house."

"What's the rush?"

"We want to hang signs around town right away. And we're hoping you can get the newspaper—the *Pilot*—to run an ad or something."

"You mean a classified." Melissa thought for a minute, maybe two. It felt like an hour to Nico. Finally she said, "I'm in!"

THURSDAY—PLAN A IN ACTION

Nico knocked on the shed door three times quickly, then waited and knocked twice more. "Secret knock," he told Melissa.

Lili opened the door with Spunky in her arms. "Spunky, this is Nicholas and his sister Melissa. She's going to take your picture."

Lili put Spunky on a chair and posed her.

"She is beyond cute," Melissa said looking at the puppy through her camera lens. She snapped a bunch of photos. "I'll develop them as soon as we get back home and send them right to the *Pilot* for the ad. If we're lucky, they'll

run it in tomorrow's paper and all through the weekend."
Melissa smiled, then remembered: "I'll give Nico a bunch,
too, so you all can make posters."

"How will we know if anyone recognizes her?" Lili asked.

Melissa had the answer. "People will call or email the
newspaper. That's how classified ads work. I'll tell them to
send any responses to me."

"What about the posters?" Nico asked.

"I think the *Pilot* will let us put their email on the
poster, too."

"Wow! You've thought of everything. Thank you
Lissa. Maybe by Monday, Spunky will be back at her home."

"I hope so," Melissa said.

THE WEEKEND—BUSY!

The kids were busy from after school on Friday right through Sunday, making posters and hanging them all over town. Every time Hannah taped a poster to a pole or tacked it on a bulletin board she said, "That Spunky—she really is the cutest!"

"Even more in person. Or in dog, I guess," Nico said.

Hannah groaned. "In dog?" Everyone laughed.

When the last poster was up, Hannah said, "That's almost fifty posters everywhere possible."

Meanwhile, Brandon's older brother Michael was

taking Spunky on long walks in downtown Raccoon River, keeping her out of the shed while Lili's parents were at home. Michael asked anyone who stopped to pet Spunky, or even just looked at her, if they recognized her.

After all that work, the kids were glad that Lili had invited them to her house for lunch on Sunday. She and her mother baked every Sunday, so after their sandwiches, they were treated to still-warm snickerdoodles.

Mrs. Tucker looked at each of them. "It's so great to be with you all again. Of course, we see a lot of Brandon. He walks Lili to and from school every day. But I haven't seen Nico and Hannah since the big opening of the Plaza Theater. And it's nice to meet you, Michael and Melissa, the older Raccoon River Kids. Are you working on anything special now?"

The kids looked at each other. No one answered. Lili's mom answered her own question: "I guess it's not something you can talk about."

"Not yet, Mrs. Tucker," Brandon said. Nico, Hannah,

and Lili nodded, and Lili repeated, "Not yet, Mom."

As soon as they left Lili's house, each with a package of cookies in hand, Hannah said, "That felt yucky. This keeping-a-secret stuff is hard! Mrs. Tucker is so nice. Are we sure she won't let Lili keep Spunky?"

"That's what Lili says. But I'll ask again," Brandon answered.

"Let's hope that the posters and the ad work, and Spunky's family calls. Soon!"

But by Sunday night, there had been no calls to the *Pilot*, and the situation was exactly where it had been. No progress, no clues. The only thing that had changed was that Lili had gotten even more attached to Spunky. Sure, she knew she couldn't keep the dog, but she was glad she had more time with her.

"We're going to have to come up with a Plan B," Hannah said. "Just in case…"

MONDAY—PLAN B

Monday was warm for the start of April. Classes lined up in the yard instead of in the cafeteria, so Brandon, Hannah, and Nico had a little extra time to share ideas before the line monitor blew her whistle.

Hannah had a good idea. "If we can't find Spunky's old family, we're going to have to find her a new one. We can write a bunch of notes—a very lot of notes!—about a puppy needing a home and hand them out to kids at school. We'll have to be careful so teachers don't see them."

"But what if someone wants the dog? How will the kid know how to reach us?" Brandon asked.

"I thought of that," Hannah said. "The notes will tell anyone interested to leave a message taped to the bottom of cafeteria table 4. We'll pick up the messages at the end of the day."

"That's real spy stuff," Nico said and high-fived Hannah.

"Could work," Brandon said.

"Meanwhile, maybe somebody will see our posters and call the *Pilot*," Nico said hopefully.

The line-up whistle interrupted them, and they joined their classmates.

At lunch, the three friends wrote notes.

PUPPY NEEDS A HOME!
IF YOU'RE INTERESTED, TAPE A MESSAGE
TO THE BOTTOM OF TABLE 4 IN THE
CAFETERIA. WE'LL CONTACT YOU.

When the lunch bell rang, Brandon quickly counted up the notes. They had twenty. Not a bad start. He divided the pile among the three of them. When the kids got back to their classrooms, they started giving the notes out.

At the end of the school day, Hannah slipped into the cafeteria to check under table 4. Uh-oh! All the tables had been moved into one corner of the cafeteria so the room would be wide open for after-school activities. All the table numbers were stuffed into a box.

So much for that plan.

When Lili got home from school, Spunky was definitely not living up to her name. She barely lifted her head when Lili walked in. She had not finished her food. Lili gently lifted Spunky onto her lap. "Don't worry. Everything will be fine. You'll see."

Lili rubbed Spunky's belly. "Are you sick?" she asked the dog.

Lili went back to the house. Her dad was at the computer in the den. *Could I ask him to take a look at Spunky*, she wondered. Brandon had said that her father might help them. Maybe now was the time.

But before she could say anything, her dad asked, "What was the best thing in school today?" He asked that every day.

Lili had her answer ready: "I drew a new cover for

a book the librarian read to us. It was called *Harry the Dirty Dog*." Lili went on. "Harry is a white dog with black spots. One day he goes out on his own. He finds all kinds of messes to get into, and when he finally gets back home, he is a black dog with white spots. His family doesn't even recognize him."

"I remember that book," Lili's dad said, smiling. "Grandma used to read it to me."

Lili was ready to blurt out everything about Spunky to her dad. She needed his help, especially if Spunky was sick. But where should she begin? Instead, she took a breath and asked if she could go over to Brandon's house.

She caught Brandon as he was pulling his bicycle out of the garage.

"Wait, Brandon." He stopped. Lili looked down and reported, "Spunky's sick."

"What do you mean by sick?" Brandon said.

Lili described how Spunky was acting. "Maybe she's just worried," she added.

"I'm on my way to Nico's. We'll figure something out. I'll stop by later."

Brandon told Nico and Hannah that Spunky was sick.

"Something like this was sure to happen," Hannah said. "It's been three days already, and we are not any closer to finding Spunky a home. No one answered the ad in the newspaper. We don't know for sure, but I don't think anyone at school answered our notes. And now this sick thing. We don't know how to take care of her. There's got to be someone we can trust who knows more about taking care of animals than we do."

Brandon turned to Hannah. "Don't you have a pet?"

"Goldfish," Hannah answered softly.

"Just goldfish?"

"Yes. I feed them—a pinch or two of fish food—every night. My mom helps me clean the tank once a week. That's about it."

"We have a dog," said Brandon. "Roxie. My dad left her. She's a good dog, but all I do is walk her. My mom and brother feed her and take care of all the other stuff."

"I bet Roxie has a veterinarian," Hannah said.

"Right. She does. He's not in Raccoon River, though. He's at the animal hospital in Franklin."

"That's far. We can't get Spunky there. Without a grown-up, I mean," Hannah said.

"Maybe we could call the vet's office. They might help us over the phone," Nico suggested.

"There are three, maybe four, doctors," Brandon explained. "And lots of helpers. The helpers answer the phone. They might have answers for us."

"Let's do it. Can you get the phone number?" Hannah asked.

Brandon nodded. "In the meantime, we could go to the supermarket and look in the dog food aisle. There might be some kind of medicine there."

"Good thinking," Hannah said. "After school tomorrow."

It may not have been the best idea, but it was better than doing nothing.

TUESDAY—THE CHICKEN CHILDREN

When the final school bell rang, Lili wasted no time getting to the veggie garden to meet her friends.

She was out of breath when she told Brandon, Nico, and Hannah, "We don't have to go to the supermarket to look at dog food boxes. We don't have to call the animal doctor. I know this girl Gabby. She's one of those chicken children, and…"

"Slow down, Lili. Chicken children?" Brandon asked.

"Yes. You know, that club that has the farm festival every summer. The kids show off their pigs and cows and giant eggplants. And chickens. Gabby has chickens."

Hannah smiled. "The 4-H clubs. We always go. These are no regular chickens. They are gorgeous. The kids raise them and show and tell all about them."

Brandon and Nico were not convinced, but Hannah urged Lili on: "And…?"

"Gabby is in fifth grade; she knows everything about animals. I saw her in the girls' room this morning, and I told her about Spunky. She said she would come home with me today and take a look at Spunky. She'll tell us what to do. And she won't tell her mother. She promised."

"If you say so," Brandon said, still not certain this was a good plan. But Gabby was already there, standing with them.

"Let's go and see that sick pup," Gabby said.

Lili set the pace. The five kids made it to Lili's house in record time.

"Gabby and I will tell Dad that we're here. Then I'll bring Gabby to the shed. We'll meet you there."

"Aye-aye, Captain," Hannah said.

The kids had never visited Spunky all together. Hannah hadn't even met her. Spunky was sure glad to see them. Her tail started wagging like crazy as soon as they opened the door.

"Awww," Hannah said. "Look at her perky little ears. And those sparkly eyes. I know why Lili's in love with her!"

"Come here, girl," Nico called to the dog. She ran across the shed floor and slid right into Nico's feet. "She's a big ball of energy."

Just then, Gabby and Lili joined them in the shed. Spunky jumped right into Lili's arms. She held the dog out to Gabby.

"What do you think, Gabby?" she asked.

Gabby took a good look, rubbed Spunky's belly, felt her nose and then announced that there was nothing— nothing at all—wrong with this dog. "She is 100% healthy. She was probably just scared and lonely all day long in the dark shed. She needs time outside. She needs to run. Do

you have some toys you can leave with her while you're in

school? A couple of balls? A sturdy chew toy? That would

help keep her happy."

"We can do that," Nico said.

"We have some tennis balls in the garage," Lili said.

"There are some brand new chew toys for Roxie at

home. I'll pick the smallest ones and bring them over later," Brandon said.

"That should do the trick," Gabby said.

"Meanwhile," Hannah added, "if any of your friends at 4-H want a puppy, it looks like we've got one that needs a home."

"No responses to the posters? Or from the ad?" Gabby asked.

"Nothing," Hannah said.

"Nothing at all," Brandon said.

"Okay then, I'll spread the word," Gabby said as she headed out of the shed door.

"We're lucky that Spunky isn't sick. What would we do if she were?" Hannah wondered after Gabby left.

"There's an animal shelter in Middleton. But how can we get there without a grown-up to drive us?"

Brandon said.

"Maybe Ms. Allen will drive us? She loves it when she and her class get involved with our projects," Nico suggested.

"Or we could ask the librarian. Mr. Fredericks was so helpful when I needed information about the Plaza Theater," Hannah said hopefully.

"Without telling Lili's parents? Without telling *all* of our parents? Grown-ups aren't going to like this secret stuff," Brandon warned.

"There you go again, Brandon," Hannah complained. "Mr. Negative. Mr. Bad News."

"Hannah, that's not fair. You know it's true," Nico said.

"We can keep hoping that Spunky's owners show up, but in the meantime, we have to try harder to find a new home for Spunky. We have to do *something*," Hannah said.

Brandon tried to gauge the expression on Lili's face. "What do you think, Lili?"

"You're right. And soon! I'm worried that my mom and dad are going to want to get into the shed soon. It's been so nice and warm. They said something about taking out the picnic table and setting it up outside."

Lili was saying the right thing, but the kids knew she really didn't want to find Spunky a home. Not anymore. She wanted to keep Spunky. Lili cuddled the dog while rocking on an old garden chair. She was getting sad and scared all at once.

"What we need is one super, can't-fail idea," said Nico. "One way to introduce Spunky to lots of people. Someone's going to want her."

The shed got very quiet as the four kids concentrated hard, hunting, hunting, hunting for that one great idea.

But guess who had an idea of her own?

Spunky wriggled out of Lili's arms, jumped down from the chair, took a running start, and performed a somersault. Then she sat down and looked up at the children.

Lili and Hannah, Nico and Brandon applauded

and cheered.

"Did you know Spunky could do tricks?"

Lili shook her head.

Hannah stood up. "Tricks. Doggie tricks. We should hold a big pet show in the park. We'll invite kids to bring their pets and have a parade. We'll bring Spunky and show her off."

Nico completed her idea: "At the end of the parade, we can announce that Spunky needs a home. By then, she will have won lots of fans, don't you think? Maybe her own first family will be there."

"That's it! Absolutely!" Hannah said.

Brandon was too excited to sit still. "We can also tell people that Raccoon River needs an animal shelter of its own."

"Our parents will find out," Hannah said. "But they'll be having so much fun, they won't be angry. Well, maybe a little angry."

Lili got caught up in the idea. She knew Spunky needed a home, and what a great way of finding just the right one. "When can we do it?" Lili asked.

"How about Sunday afternoon?" Brandon suggested.

"What will we call it? Pet Parade doesn't sound like a big deal. We need a better name," said Hannah. "Something BIG. Something NEW. Something FUN."

"How about PET LALAPALOOZA," Nico said. "I saw that word on a book cover in the library."

"Catchy!" Hannah said.

"Cool," Brandon agreed.

Lili said, "I went to a petting zoo one time. They had lambs and calves and chicks and piglets. It was so much fun. We could call it a Petting Zoo and Parade."

"Too many words," Brandon said. "But Zoo is a great start. Zoo something."

"How about Zooapalooza?"

Brandon, Hannah, and Nico looked at Lili. How did she come up with stuff like that?

"Catchier," Hannah said.

"Coolest!"

"Done!"

And that was Lili's final word on the subject.

WEDNESDAY—GATHERING THE PIECES

Lili counted. Only four days to the Zooapalooza. It was the first thing she said to Brandon when he picked her up for school that morning.

"Four days."

"Yup."

"Can we really make this happen?" Lili asked.

"I'm sure Hannah's got lists ready for us. We'll be busy, but yes, we will make it happen. That's what the Raccoon River Kids do."

Sure enough, Hannah had lists. Nico was going to call the mayor to get permission to use the park on Sunday.

Hannah was going to call the community center to borrow chairs and stage set-ups, and maybe a tent or two. Brandon had to call the vet's office in Franklin and ask if they could help. Melissa was going to persuade the *Raccoon River Pilot* to run free ads inviting families to bring their pets. Lili's job was to convince the kindergarten and first-grade teachers to give their classes time to make signs about the Zooapalooza to hang all over town.

When the end-of-day bell rang, the kids raced home and made their calls.

Nico grabbed Mayor Wilson's card from his bulletin board. This was not the first time he had made a call like this, but it wasn't any easier now. After all, he was calling a pretty important guy: his town's mayor! But there was no time to waste. He punched the numbers into the phone.

The same woman answered as the last time.

"Hello, this is Nicholas Preston. Do you remember me?"

"Why yes, of course! You and your pals have done a lot for Raccoon River. Is there something new going on?"

"Yes. May I talk with Mayor Wilson please?"

"I'm afraid not," the woman said. "He is out of town until next week."

"Oh." Nicholas was not expecting that. Now what?

"Maybe I can help you. I'm Mrs. Warner, the mayor's assistant. What do you need?"

"We need to use the park for a pet parade.

On Sunday."

"Well, Nicholas, I *can* help with that. I make all the reservations for the use of the park by citizens' groups. I have some questions for our form. Okay if I ask them now?"

"Sure," Nico said, relieved that they wouldn't have to postpone the Zooapalooza.

"When is the parade?"

"Sunday."

"Yes, you told me that. Which Sunday?"

"This Sunday."

"This Sunday?"

"Yup."

"That's awfully short notice. Someone else might have already reserved the space."

Nico heard her turning pages. They hadn't thought about this. What if someone else was using the park that day?

But when Mrs. Warner got back on the phone, she said, "What a stroke of luck. There are no reservations for this weekend. Now, how long will the parade last?"

"From two until four."

"How many people do you think will be there?"

"I don't know. We are inviting kids and their pets and their families."

"So we'll need Sanitation to be there. Pets, well, you know... I hope Sanitation doesn't have other events they have to cover."

Again, Nico heard more pages being turned. He held his breath.

"You're a lucky fella," Mrs. Warner said. "They are available."

"Whew. We didn't think about that."

"That's okay. That's my job. Back to the size of the crowd. Can you take a guess?"

When Nico didn't answer, she asked, "Less than the number that would fill the Plaza Theater?"

"Much less."

"What if I guessed at 99 people? That way we don't

have to have Medical on hand. And since it's outdoors, we don't need the fire department. But you will need the police there. At least one officer." She paused, then said, "I forgot to ask. You won't be selling food or beverages, will you?"

"No."

"Just about done. Who will pay for the permit and for the town workers?"

This was the hardest question of all. They didn't have any money.

When Nico didn't answer, she prompted, "Nico?"

"We didn't think we would have to pay. We're just doing this ourselves – you know, just the Raccoon River Kids."

"Maybe your parents could get together and cover these costs. It isn't a lot of money."

Nico thought fast. "No. This is…um…this is a surprise."

"Oh, a surprise for your parents! Lovely." Mrs. Warner thought for a moment, then said, "Hmmmm. The Mayor has a small fund to support local groups. I think he'd want me to use some of it for this."

"Really?"

"I'm certain. You all have proven yourselves to be outstanding young citizens."

"Thank you. Thank you. You are so nice!"

"I'll issue the permit. Since time is so tight, you won't actually have the printed permit until after the parade. If you are bringing in chairs or tables or anything like that, just tell the folks who are delivering them that the permit is in progress. They can call this office to double check if they wish."

"WOW. By the way, we're calling this Zooapalooza. We think it sounds more exciting than plain old Pet Parade."

"Zooapalooza," Mrs. Warner repeated. "Great name! Good luck, Nico. Maybe I'll see you at the park on Sunday."

Nico took a big breath. That was a whole lot harder than he expected, but things worked out. He called Hannah and told her about the permit. She would need to let the people at the community center know that they had one, so they could deliver the chairs and tables.

"Piece of cake," Hannah told him. "They asked me if we had a permit. I told them you were talking to Mayor Wilson. They knew he'd give us the permit."

"Not really cake," Nico said. "She had so many questions!"

"But you got it covered, right?"

"Did you talk to Brandon?" Nico asked.

"I did. The people at the veterinarian's office were glad to know about our plans. They have a college student there who is studying to be a vet. He's going to help us. First thing, he's going to visit Lili and Spunky and help her get Spunky ready."

"Looking good," Nico said.

THURSDAY—INTO THE COUNTDOWN

Three days until Zooapalooza.

According to Hannah's plan, this was the day to get schoolmates and friends involved.

Brandon worked the morning line-up, talking to all the groups in the school yard, asking kids if they have a pet, and if they'd like to show and tell about their pet at the Zooapalooza.

Marty, a boy in the fourth grade, had a parrot named Pete who talked.

"Pete?"

"Yes. We named him that because he repeats what

you say."

"Ha ha ha. Re-Pete," Brandon said. "He's got to be one of our stars."

Marty agreed. He would ask his parents if the family could bring Pete to the park on Sunday.

That's one, Brandon said to himself.

Brandon saw Gabby and told her about the big event.

"The 4-H sets up all kinds of pet activities at fairs and stuff," she told Brandon. "We could do that at the Zooapalooza. And I could give a demonstration with one of my chickens."

"Fantastic," Brandon said. "We have some tents available. Your 4-H club could set up in one of them."

"Deal," Gabby said. "My uncle is one of the club leaders. I'm sure he'll want us to be a part of this."

"Thanks, Gabby."

That's two, Brandon counted.

A girl in the sixth grade had built a hamster habitat for her pet. She was happy to have a chance to explain how she did it and show it off. And a second-grader had a cat who played a toy piano, sort of.

"Why not," Brandon told him.

That's four. Not bad, Brandon thought.

Nico and Hannah went around the cafeteria tables at lunchtime, telling kids how much fun they would have at the park on Sunday afternoon. They should tell their parents about it and bring their pets.

"There will be lots to do and see. Please come."

Lili told her teacher. "Can I bring my dog?" Mr. Adams asked.

"Of course. That's the point," Lili said.

Mr. Adams announced to the whole class that he and his dog Elvis would be at the Zooapalooza in the park on Sunday. He hoped to see lots of his students there. Elvis wanted to meet them.

After school, Lili went straight to the shed so she could get Spunky ready for the big day. She wasn't sure what she should do, but Brandon had given her a brush. She brushed Spunky so her hair would shine.

Lili heard a sound at the shed door and peeked out to see what it was. A teenager was standing there. It must be the guy Brandon told her would be stopping by from the veterinarian's office in Franklin.

"Lili?" he asked, when she opened the door just a crack. "I'm Tristan, from Franklin Veterinary. I'm here to help with Spunky and the Zooapalooza."

Lili opened the door a little more, and Tristan saw the dog. "Hello there, Spunky," he said. "You're the reason for all these big doings, aren't you?" He knelt down to pet the dog.

"She likes you," Lili told him.

"I like her too. Have you thought about what she can do when you introduce her to the audience on Sunday?"

Lili shook her head. She wasn't sure what Tristan meant.

"Can Spunky show off some tricks, so people will see how clever she is?"

"She can do somersaults."

"That's cool. Anything else?"

Lili shrugged. "I don't think so."

"Let's try," Tristan encouraged. He stood right in front of Spunky and said "Sit."

Spunky sat.

"Lie down."

Spunky did.

"Roll over."

Spunky obeyed.

Tristan got on his knees and rubbed the top of Spunky's head and her ears. "Good dog."

"Crawl," Tristan commanded.

Spunky stood still.

"That's one she doesn't know. Let's teach her. Do you have any treats?"

Lili got a handful of dog treats, and she and Tristan taught Spunky how to crawl.

"That will make a good show on Sunday—those four commands plus a somersault, and she'll have everyone there wanting to take her home."

"Everyone?" Lili repeated, looking very worried. She knew Tristan was on her side. Could she trust him with her fears? She tried: "What if the Zooapalooza works? What if Spunky's old family sees her there and wants to take her back?"

"Would that be a bad thing?" Tristan asked.

"That would be okay, I guess. But what if a whole other family wants to take Spunky home? That would be hard. Who are they, this family that wants my dog? They could be mean. Maybe they won't take care of her. Do they even have children to play with Spunky?"

"We will all make sure Spunky gets a great family."

After Tristan left, Lili picked up Spunky. "He knows stuff," she told the puppy. "If Tristan says we're going to find you a great home, then we will!"

How would Lili ever keep that promise?

FRIDAY—THIS CLOSE

There were four children at Raccoon River Elementary School who were having a hard time paying attention in class on Friday. Zooapalooza was *this close*, and there were a bunch of last minute things they had to do. Could they get it done?

Nico and Hannah were worried. Brandon kept their spirits up. He was sure that if any problems came up, they'd be able to work them out. "We always do."

But the moment Brandon came home from school, he stepped right into a problem he couldn't figure out. There

were three stuffed duffel bags on the kitchen floor. His
mother was packing ice and tons of food into the cooler.
Roxie wasn't barking.

"Hey Mom, what's all this? Where's Roxie?"

"Oh, Brandon! I had a great idea. The weather is
supposed to be perfect, so I thought we'd get away this

weekend—just you and your brother and me. The Jacksons are looking after Roxie."

"Huh? Just like that? Without any plans? All of a sudden?"

"What's all of a sudden?" Michael said when he walked into the conversation.

"I rented a cabin in Vermont. About three hours from here. It's not exactly roughing it, like we used to do, but we'll be in the woods, we'll cook outside…*And* we'll have indoor plumbing."

Brandon listened quietly. He knew his family needed some time together—away from his mother's job, and from schoolwork, and house chores, and arguments over whose turn it was to take the garbage out. Just getting ready for the trip, his mother already seemed happier than she had been for a long time. Since his father left. He couldn't let her down.

But what about Hannah and Nico? And Lili. Lili! He couldn't disappoint them either.

"Something's bothering you Brandon," his mother said. "What's wrong?"

"I sort of had plans."

"What kind of plans?"

"With my friends."

"Are they plans you can postpone? Until next weekend?"

Brandon shook his head and said softly, "Not really."

"I went to a lot of trouble to surprise you boys. I know we'll have fun. We always enjoyed our weekends in the woods."

When Dad was still home, the Keefer family would sometimes throw stuff into the car and take off. They drove until they found what looked like a perfect spot to set up camp. Usually it was.

But why did Mom have to pick *this* weekend? Brandon looked at his brother for help. After all, Michael knew all about the Zooapalooza. Michael shrugged his shoulders and mouthed the words "tell her."

Maybe Michael was right. Maybe Brandon should tell her about Lili and Spunky and the can't-fail plan that the Raccoon River Kids had finally come up with. She would understand—probably.

No. This was a secret. He couldn't break his word.

Except that explaining it was the only way. This was complicated.

Brandon decided that he *had* to explain it all to his mother. He told her the whole story—about Lili and Spunky and the Zooapalooza. Everything.

"Zooapalooza. I saw posters about it in a couple of store windows," Mom said. "I've been wondering what it was. And I certainly didn't know you were involved, Brandon. This is what happens when you keep secrets."

The three of them stared at each other for a while. Finally, Michael said, "Can you get the money back for the cabin Mom? Or change the date to another weekend?"

"Can you, Mom? Would you?"

Mrs. Keefer made a couple of calls. Michael went next

door and picked up Roxie.

Brandon hugged his mom. "Thank you."

Then Brandon made a couple of phone calls of his own.

SATURDAY—COMING CLEAN

The secret was out. Hannah and Nico agreed that Brandon had no choice but to tell his mother what was going on. Otherwise, he wouldn't be at the Zooapalooza. They needed him. There was a long list of things he had to do. Plus, it wouldn't be fair if he missed the big finale to this latest adventure.

Hannah figured it was time to tell her parents about Spunky and how Lili and Hannah, Nico and Brandon had kept her a secret.

Nico did the same.

The parents were angry.

"You should have told us," Mrs. Levin said to Hannah. "Maybe we could have helped. We don't like it when you keep things from us."

Hannah expected that, but she saw that her parents were also proud. They talked about loyalty and friendship. Nico's parents even praised the clever ways the kids handled problems as they came up.

Then all three kids went to Lili's house and, along with Lili, confessed to her parents.

"I thought something was going on," Mr. Tucker said. "When you came by with Gabby the other day, something seemed a little out of kilter."

While everyone was talking, Brandon slipped out, went to the shed, picked up Spunky, and carried her back to the living room, whispering to the dog. "Now it's time for you to be your very cutest. You have to win over Lili's mom."

Brandon put Spunky into Mr. Tucker's arms. "Awww," he said. "She's adorable."

That was easy. Of course, they already knew that Lili's dad liked dogs. Everyone turned to Lili's mom. What did she think?

Lili took a deep breath.

Hannah closed her eyes, crossed her fingers, and made a wish.

Nico did all he could to stop his feet from tapping.

Brandon spoke up: "She's a good dog. Lili loves her. And the rest of us will help to take care of her if only she can stay."

Mrs. Tucker walked slowly toward her husband, bent down to have a good look into Spunky's face. She lifted the dog from Mr. Tucker's lap, held her close, and said: "Spunky, eh?"

"Yes!" all four kids said at once. "Spunky!"

"Just like me, Mommy," Lili added.

No one spoke. No one even moved. They watched Lili's mom holding the dog, rubbing her ears, scratching her back, and they saw something spark between the two of

them. Spunky put her head down on Mrs. Tucker's shoulder and nuzzled into her neck.

Mrs. Tucker smiled. "She's lovely."

But would she let Lili keep the dog?

Mrs. Tucker looked at each of the children—Brandon, then Nico and Hannah, and last, Lili. "I'm sure she'll find a great home on Sunday. She is hard to resist."

It was like a balloon popped inside every one of the

Raccoon River Kids' chests. Brandon put his arm around Lili's shoulders. "We never expected your family to keep Spunky," he reminded her. "It was nice to think it might happen, but it didn't. So, it's on to the Zooapalooza."

Lili held back her tears. "Guess so."

Lili was excited, nervous, hopeful, worried, and just plain scared. How was it going to feel to leave Zooapalooza without Spunky? That was probably what was going to happen. Tomorrow!

She was sure she would never get to sleep. It would be better if she could bring Spunky to her room—just for this one night, this one last night.

"No, Lili. I don't think it would be wise."

"Please Mommy. PLEEZE."

"Let's just leave things as they are, Lili."

Lili got into bed and tried about a thousand different

ways to get comfortable. Tucking the covers in to make
a cozy sleeping bag. Climbing on top of the covers and
pulling one half over her. Sleeping on her stomach, her side,
her back, her other side. Sleeping with her head at the foot
of the bed. Sleeping across the bed. Bringing all her stuffed
animals into bed with her. One pillow. One pillow folded
over. Two pillows. No pillows.

She must have fallen asleep, at least for a while,
because the next thing Lili knew, the sky was getting lighter.

It was Sunday morning.

SUNDAY MORNING—MISSING!

At 6:00 AM, Lili was dressed and ready to go. She tiptoed down the stairs, quietly opened the door, and headed to the shed. This would probably be her last morning with Spunky. The last breakfast she would feed her.

Spunky wasn't in her bed. She wasn't curled up on the old sofa that used to be in the living room. Lili looked around, in every corner, under every piece of furniture, behind every box. There weren't many places in the shed where Spunky could hide.

"Spunky. Come here, girl." Lili waited and listened. She called again a little louder. "Spunky!" Then again, louder still.

Where was Spunky?

The door to the shed had been latched shut, hadn't it? Lili thought hard. Had she unlocked the door or simply pulled it open? It was barely a minute ago. Why couldn't she remember how she got into the shed? Did she turn the knob on the latch to open it or just pull the handle? Come to think of it, when she left the shed yesterday, had she latched the door? Had she even closed it tight?

If she hadn't, Spunky could have pushed the door open. Yes, she was pretty small, but she could be very determined. All Spunky needed was a little crack of space to get out.

That must have been what happened. Now Spunky was gone. She had run away!

Lili rushed outside. "Spunky. Spunky. Come here, Spunky." Lili shook a box of dog food. "Here's your breakfast. Come and get it, girl."

Spunky did not come from around the house. She did

not step out from the woods. She did not run to Lili from the neighbor's yard.

Lili hurried to the house and climbed the steps to her parents' bedroom as fast as she could.

"Spunky's run away," she announced as she tapped hard on her father's shoulder. "She's gone."

"What?" said Mommy. "What do you mean?"

"I mean Spunky left. And do you know why she left? It's because she doesn't want to go to the Zooapalooza and then have to go home with another family. It's because she likes it here. She likes my friends. She loves me. She wants this to be her home. But you won't let that happen. That's why she ran away. It's all because of you."

Lili's face was red. Tears running down her cheeks. Her voice was cracking. She was sniffling. She collapsed on the edge of her parents' bed, exhausted.

Her mother said nothing.

"Where have you looked?" Daddy asked.

Lili tried to answer, but she had the crying hiccups.

"All…hiccup…all over…hiccup…the shed. And, and, and in the backyard…big hiccup."

"She might have wandered next door," Mommy suggested.

"No. Looked there."

Lili's dad was dressed by then. "Let's take a good look outside. Show me where you usually walk Spunky."

Lili led her dad outside while her mom grabbed the phone.

"Marilyn, this is Lili's mom, Jill Tucker. Lili's dog has gone missing. I thought she might be at your place. She knows Brandon."

"So I heard, but just on Friday. They really kept this adventure quiet, huh?"

Lili's mother agreed. "They did. Have you seen Spunky?"

"I haven't. Let me ask Brandon. If he knows anything, I'll call you back right away."

"Thank you."

Brandon was sitting outside at the picnic table. There was a dog on his lap. Spunky!

"Brandon, the Tucker family is going crazy looking for that little dog. How long have you had her?"

"I don't know when she got here. She was sitting under the table—shaking, scared, covered in dirt and dust—when I went out to pick up the *Pilot*. After all that brushing that Lili did yesterday."

"I'm going to call Lili's mother now. Will you please take the dog back?"

"I was going to, but I thought I should wait awhile. It isn't even seven o'clock yet."

"They are all up."

"On my way."

As soon as Lili knew that Brandon had Spunky, she ran to meet him.

"Oh no," Lili said the moment she caught a glimpse of Spunky in Brandon's arms. "She's a mess. What was she doing?"

"Must have been exploring," Brandon answered. "Nothing that some brushing won't fix."

Lili didn't really care how Spunky looked. She was overjoyed that Spunky was safe. "Oh, Spunky," she whispered. "I thought you were gone. I'm so glad you're okay."

Lili carried Spunky the rest of the way home, took out her brush, and started the cleanup. Her mom put food and water into Spunky's bowls. Lili's dad watched the two of them as they cared for Spunky.

By 11:30, the Tuckers, with Spunky in the lead, got into their car and headed for the park.

"Mommy," Lili said, leaning toward the front seat, "I didn't mean to yell at you or say all those things."

"You were scared, Lili. I know," said her mom.

"I was. But it wasn't your fault."

Lili's mom turned around and winked at Lili and Spunky. Lili lifted the dog so she could lick her mother's hand.

"Hello there, Spunky. We're all glad you're okay. This is your special day."

The park was just ahead. Before she got out of the

car, Lili gave Spunky one last hug. Her friends would be waiting for her.

12

SUNDAY AFTERNOON—SET-UP

Brandon had already told Hannah and Nico how Spunky ran away, so when they saw Lili and Spunky walking towards them, they got up for a long group hug.

"You must have been so scared," Nico said to Lili.

"I was. And sad, too," Lili said. "I think Spunky ran away because she didn't want to go home from the Zooapalooza with another family."

"We're all here now. It's sunny and warm. Lots of people will come. It's all good, Lili," Hannah said.

Lili bent down to pet Spunky and give her ears a scratch when she noticed something going on in the field

next to the stage.

"What's going on over there?" Lili asked, pointing to the park's big lawn. "Are people here already? Isn't this supposed to start at 2:00?"

"Let's go check it out," Hannah said.

At the edge of the field, they saw Melissa with a few of her middle-school friends, setting up a tent.

"What's this, Melissa?" Nico asked. "I didn't know

you were going to be here."

"I told Brandon. He put me in this tent. I'm setting up a pet photo studio. I think people will want to have pictures of themselves with their pets at the very first ever Raccoon River Zooapalooza."

"What a great idea," Hannah said. "People will love that."

Not far from the photo tent, Tristan was busy at a table.

"Hey Tristan. What are you doing here?"

Lili ran over to the table Tristan had set up.

"Lili, these are two friends from vet school. We're setting up an information booth to answer people's questions about their pets."

"That's terrific," Nico said.

Just a few steps away, Gabby and a bunch of her buddies from the 4-H Club were setting up games under a big 4-H banner they had hung.

"Hi, Lili," Gabby called out. "How's Spunky?"

Lili just smiled and pointed to the dog.

"Looking fine," Gabby said. "Maybe she'd like to test out our find-the-ball game?"

"Sure."

Gabby took a red ball and let Spunky sniff it a few times. She put the ball on the ground and told Spunky to pick it up. Spunky didn't seem to understand. "Like this," Gabby demonstrated. "Pick up the ball and give it to Lili." Gabby did just that. She did it again. After a moment, Spunky imitated her. Gabby rewarded Spunky with praise and a few back rubs. Spunky looked mighty pleased with herself.

Then, Gabby asked Lili to turn the dog around. Gabby hid the red ball behind a tree. "Find the ball and bring it to Lili," Gabby told Spunky. The dog hesitated. She sniffed the air and then pulled on the leash, leading Lili to the tree. Spunky didn't see the ball at first. She sniffed again and walked around the tree. There it was—the red ball. Spunky picked it up and dropped it right at Lili's feet.

"Good dog!" everyone cheered.

"Great dog," Lily corrected, getting down on her knees and hugging Spunky.

Gabby gave Spunky a treat. "We'll play with lots of dogs today. We'll keep track of the time it takes for each of them to find the ball and return it to their master. The dogs with the shortest time will be our grand prize winners."

Brandon said, "I'm going to enter Roxie. She's good at finding stuff."

One of Gabby's club friends pointed to the lawn area nearby. "This is our Frisbee field for people and their dogs. It's fun to watch them play." Near the field, she showed the kids a spot where they would set up a table for a display of prize chickens.

Gabby told the kids that another 4-H member was bringing his horse. "He's going to give little kids rides around this big lawn."

"Lili's little," one of Gabby's friends said.

"Not today. Today, Lili is one of our leaders. Right,

Lili?" Hannah asked.

"Right," Lili answered. Spunky barked her agreement.

George, another 4-H kid, showed everyone the cookies he'd baked.

"They look delicious," Brandon told George, reaching out for a sample.

"They are, but they are not for people. They are healthy snacks for dogs that I bake myself. I'll be giving them away along with the recipe, so maybe more people will make better food for their animals."

"Thank you all," Hannah said. "What you're doing will make the Zooapalooza so special!"

Brandon's mother caught up with the kids and said, "It's almost two. I brought sandwiches for you and your parents. Let's find a place for a picnic before the crowds arrive."

"Hey, don't forget something for Spunky," George called out, handing Lili one of his doggie cookies. "You don't want her to be hungry."

The kids and their parents sat in a circle and enjoyed their lunches. All of them were thinking how wonderful the Zooapalooza was turning out to be.

13

SUNDAY—ZOOAPALOOZA

The Raccoon River Kids went to their assigned places as cars began to arrive at the park: Brandon in the East Parking Lot, Nico in the West, Hannah at the park's central crossroad, all of them answering questions and giving directions. Lili greeted families at the Main Gate.

Almost everyone arrived with a pet. They had cat carriers, parakeet cages, hamster habitats, and, of course, dogs of every kind and size on leashes. One boy pulled an enormous snake in an aquarium on his wagon along the bumpy walkway.

"Gee, I hope your snake likes bumps," Lili said.

"Don't worry, he's not poison or anything."

"Oh. That's good," Lili said. "Welcome to Zooapalooza."

At three o'clock, one of the 4-H kids rang a loud cowbell, and people made their way to the chairs set up in front of the stage.

Tristan got things started. He invited Marty and his parrot to the stage.

Marty introduced himself and his parrot Pete. "Pete talks," he told the audience.

"Hello Pete," he said to the bird. "Hello Marty," the parrot answered, clear as a bell.

The audience applauded.

"Do you know where you are, Pete?" Marty asked his pet. The parrot shook his head.

"Sure you do," Marty said. "We've been here before."

The parrot looked around. He seemed confused.

"Come on Pete," Marty begged. "We practiced this."

"Park," the parrot finally said.

Marty looked at the audience. "I tried to teach him to say Zooapalooza, but we didn't have enough time. Maybe next year."

The audience laughed.

Gabby came to the stage next with one of her beautiful chickens. She put some coins on a table in front of the chicken. "Show me a penny," Gabby said. The chicken pecked at a penny, which Gabby showed to the audience. "Now show me a dime." The chicken pecked at a dime. Who knew chickens could tell the difference between a penny, a nickel, a dime, and a quarter?

Amazing.

The boy with the snake did a talk about his ball python, explaining where the snake usually lives, how long it was, and how he took care of it.

The doggie champions of the find-the-ball game took their bows. A friend of Melissa had a dog who sang, and another middle-school kid had a cat who walked backwards.

At last, Tristan called Lili and Spunky to center

stage. Lili told the audience that Spunky would be demonstrating behaviors.

Lili lifted Spunky to a table and asked her to sit, lie down, roll over, and crawl. Then Lili put Spunky on the floor and said, "Somersault." Spunky took a running start and did not just one, but a double somersault, then jumped right into Lili's arms and licked her face. The audience cheered.

Brandon, Hannah, and Nico joined Lili on stage.

"Spunky is a very special dog," Brandon began. "In fact, she is the reason behind this whole Zooapalooza. It actually was her idea."

"That's true," Hannah said. "When we couldn't figure out how to find a home for Spunky, she did a somersault, and that gave us the idea."

Nico said, "Spunky needs a family, and we didn't know how to find one for her. We couldn't bring her to a shelter, because we don't have one in Raccoon River. We couldn't even bring her to a vet's office. We don't have our own in Raccoon River."

Lili picked up Spunky. "We have to fix that, don't you think?"

Just about everyone in the audience stood up, clapping and raising their arms and shouting, "YES! WE DO!"

Tristan stepped up and asked everyone to call the town

council and the mayor and anyone else who could help.

The folks in the audience started talking to one another, leaning forward to the row ahead and turning around to the family behind. It looked like the town of Raccoon River was set to make some changes.

Gabby rang the cowbell once more to quiet the crowd.

"What about Spunky? Is there a family who wants to meet her?"

No response for a minute. For two minutes. Then one hand was raised in a back row and another on the side in the second row.

Gabby led the fellow in the back row toward the stage. Tristan helped the woman in the second row move to the center.

Lili watched them approach, step by step. "Mommy!" she shouted when she recognized the woman making her way to the stage.

"And it's your dad," Brandon said, when he realized who was walking forward from the back.

"Really?" Lili yelled. "REALLY?"

Her mother and father were nodding and smiling. "Yes," was all Lili heard over the applause and shouts of the audience.

YES!

End.